I loved my grandfather.
He took me for long walks in the woods.

He knew how to make willow twigs into whistles.

He could even pull coins from behind my ear.

But he can't do those things anymore, because now he is gone.
When my parents told me Grampa was gone, I got mad. I wanted to know where he went—and why he didn't take me with him.

"You don't understand," said my mother. "Your grandfather is dead.
He died last night."
I started to cry.

Later, after I was done crying, I went to look for my mother. She was changing my sister's diaper.

"Where did Grampa go when he died?" I asked.

"I don't know," my mother answered. She looked like she was going to cry herself.

"Why don't you know?" I asked, feeling scared.

"Nobody knows for sure where you go when you die. But I can tell you what I think. I don't think Grampa has stopped being. I think he has gone to another place."

"What other place?"

She shook her head and said, "I don't know." Her voice sounded funny. She handed me the baby. "Watch Pook for a minute," she told me. Then she went into her bedroom.

I played with Pook. But all the time I was thinking of Grampa. I wanted to go find him. Only I didn't know if I wanted to go to that other place or not.

After supper I asked my father if he knew where Grampa had gone.

When he got a sad look on his face, I said, "Don't cry! Just tell me where he is."

My father closed his eyes. "Your grandfather went where we all go when we die," he said at last.

"But where is that?"

He shook his head. I could see that he didn't know.

I went next door to see my friend Mike. "Where do people go when they die?" I asked him.

"They go to the graveyard."

Now I was really confused. And scared, too. I had seen the graveyard. But I had never seen anybody there.

I wanted to go for a walk. Only I couldn't go into the woods without Grampa. So I climbed a tree instead. I sat in the branches and tried to think. Nothing made any sense.

Later I found a willow twig. I tried to make it into a whistle to call
my grandfather home. But I didn't know how. Grampa hadn't taught me
yet.

I went back inside and tried to pull a coin from behind Pook's ear. But I couldn't make the trick work. Grampa had never showed me the way to do it.

The next day my parents made me dress up. We took Pook to the baby-sitter. Then we drove to a big white house called a funeral home, to see Grampa one last time.

I was confused again. I couldn't understand how we could see him if he was gone.

"You'll have to be quiet in the funeral home," said my father.

He was right. Inside the home everyone walked softly and talked in whispers. It was so quiet it was frightening.

I didn't see any other children. I did see a lot of old people. Some of them were crying, which made me want to cry, too.

"Let's go see your grandfather," said my father.

He led me into a big room. At one end of the room was a long, shiny wooden box surrounded by a wall of flowers—more flowers than I had ever seen indoors. The sweet smell made my stomach twist a little.

My father said the box was called a coffin. He said my grandfather was inside it.

I felt funny.

My father took my hand. I held on tight. Together we walked to the coffin.

Dad was right. My grandfather was inside. He had on a suit and tie. His eyes were closed. His hands were folded across his chest.

But something was missing. This was not really my grandfather. The Grampa I knew was soft and wrinkly. This Grampa looked smooth and hard, and some of his wrinkles were gone.

My father took my hand in his. Then he put it on Grampa's hand. Grampa's fingers felt cool and smooth, not warm like they should have.

Finally I understood.

This used to be my grandfather's house.

But Grampa doesn't live here anymore.

Someday I will leave my house behind, just like my grandfather did. When that happens, I will go to look for him, because I love him very much.

I don't think it will happen for a long time.

And I don't worry about it now, because I know the house I live in isn't me.

I am not the house.

Someday I will know more.

But that's enough for now.

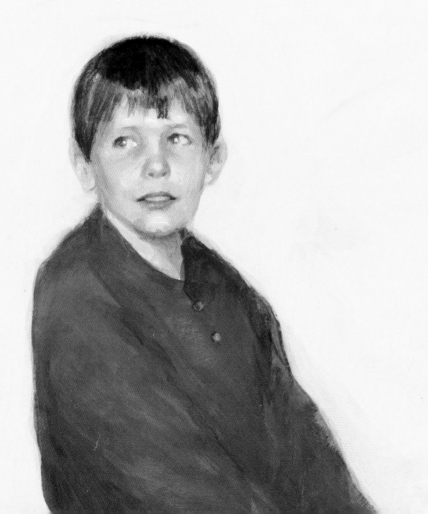